# Chorus of Bells

PRAISE FOR *STORYSHARES*

"One of the brightest innovators and game-changers in the education industry."
– Forbes

"Your success in applying research-validated practices to promote literacy serves as a valuable model for other organizations seeking to create evidence-based literacy programs."
- Library of Congress

"We need powerful social and educational innovation, and Storyshares is breaking new ground. The organization addresses critical problems facing our students and teachers. I am excited about the strategies it brings to the collective work of making sure every student has an equal chance in life."
– Teach For America

"Around the world, this is one of the up-and-coming trailblazers changing the landscape of literacy and education."
- International Literacy Association

"It's the perfect idea. There's really nothing like this. I mean wow, this will be a wonderful experience for young people."    - Andrea Davis Pinkney, Executive Director, Scholastic

"Reading for meaning opens opportunities for a lifetime of learning. Providing emerging readers with engaging texts that are designed to offer both challenges and support for each individual will improve their lives for years to come. Storyshares is a wonderful start."
- David Rose, Co-founder of CAST & UDL

# Chorus of Bells

Natalie Walker

STORYSHARES

Story Share, Inc.
New York. Boston. Philadelphia

Storyshares
Story Share, Inc.
24 N. Bryn Mawr Avenue #340
Bryn Mawr, PA 19010-3304
www.storyshares.org

*Inspiring reading with a new kind of book.*

**Interest Level:** Middle School
**Grade Level Equivalent:** 4.4

9781642611403

Book design by Storyshares

Printed in the United States of America

Storyshares Presents

# 1

None of the villagers warned him the graveyard shift would be silent. They'd stressed the intensity of the darkness, but it was the silence that overwhelmed Lester now. It swallowed him up. He felt as if he was getting smaller and smaller, drowning inside his own consciousness.

"There's a difference between quiet and silence," he reflected aloud. At least he could use his own voice to interrupt the void of nothing.

Trudging through the woods on his way to the cemetery, Lester was guided by the glow of the full moon. Twigs and dry grass crunched beneath his feet. The dim light made the trees appear to be monsters huddled in groups, planning their attack. A chilly breeze ruffled the leaves. Lester shivered. This night could not end soon enough.

It was a fortnight ago when the townsfolk called upon young men to start patrolling the graveyard at night. The widow of the town's recently deceased pastor claimed to have seen her husband's ghost roaming their house at night. After much debate, the grave was unearthed and the coffin opened. A local doctor performed a postmortem examination, searching for signs of demon possession or other supernatural elements.

Instead, he found something even more bizarre. The corpse was untouched, but the inside of the coffin was covered in scratch marks and dried blood. When the doctor examined the pastor's fingernails, though, they were clean. His findings put many townsfolk on edge. Some believed their loved ones were being buried alive, while others feared a sinister force had taken possession of the cemetery.

In response, the town's mayor announced that every corpse would be attached to a bell. This would prevent people from being buried alive. If someone did wake from the dead, they would be able to ring for help. It would also settle the rumors of demon possession, the mayor thought.

This new custom of attaching bells to graves was already being practiced in many neighboring villages, with varying tales of success. Villagers spent the following days tying rope to one finger of each corpse. The rope was attached to a bell hanging from a well-grounded pole.

Then, the mayor scheduled one man to monitor the graves each night, listening for the sound of a bell. Until Lester's shift, nothing but silence had been reported.

All of this conspiracy was hogwash to Lester. He believed there could be any number of possible explanations for scratches. Maybe animals were digging around the coffin. Maybe the wood carvers swindled the widow into unknowingly buying a damaged coffin. Maybe there was no need for explanation at all.

For Lester, at least, there wasn't. He was not a superstitious young man, unlike most of the folks in his village. If a person wasn't breathing, they're dead. And when people died, they stayed dead.

Still, he volunteered to be one of the night lookouts at the graveyard. He hoped his bravery would make his father proud. It didn't.

As night lookout, his purpose was to keep his eyes and ears open for the pull of a rope or the chime of a bell. If any unfortunate souls did happen to be buried with blood still pumping through their veins, Lester needed to dig them out.

Personally, he expected nothing of particular interest to happen. It would be a silent night.

Not long into his shift, rain began to drizzle gently. Pitter-pattering drops of water replaced the silence. Occasional thunder softly grumbled in the distance. Lester took shelter beneath a tree, attempting to keep dry.

# 2

Time moved slowly, as if creeping through molasses. Lester watched the moon, desperately willing it to move deeper into the sky and trade places with the sun. Every so often, he would be startled by a gentle whooshing sound. He knew it was only the wind, but it still made the hairs on his arms stand at attention.

*Chime.*

He heard a strange noise but ignored it.

*Chime.*

There it was again.

"What was that?" Lester asked himself.

He knew the answer. It was probably just a bell swaying in the wind. Bells move when there's wind, and bells that move make a chiming noise.

*Chime.*

The noise kept repeating from the same direction.

*Chime. Chime.*

"The wind," he whispered, "It's only the wind."

*Chime. Chime.*

It was definitely the sound of a bell. Maybe the rope wasn't secure, or the pole wasn't solid.

*Chime.*

*Chime.*

*Chime.*

The sound was getting more frequent now, harder to ignore.

*Chime. Chime. Chime.*

Lester stood, deciding to investigate. Slowly and deliberately, he tiptoed toward the graveyard without a torch. Each raindrop that touched his gooseflesh sent a jolt up his spine.

As he inched closer and closer to the nearest grave, he was blind in the darkness.

Clumsily, he used his hands and feet to navigate.

"Ouch!" he yelped, stubbing his toe on a rock.

Distant lightning strikes provided illumination. Lester used those brief bolts of light to survey as much of the burial site as he could between flashes. Everything looked as expected.

When he reached the graves, he examined the bell that he believed to be the culprit. It wasn't ringing, the pole felt sturdy, and the rope was as motionless as the corpse deep below.

# 3

Just as he was about to return to his resting spot, Lester heard a different sound. It was a repetitive noise of some kind, like a heartbeat. Turning his head back and forth to pin the location, Lester realized the sound was coming from beneath him. Swiftly, he dropped to his knees and placed his ear to the ground. He listened for several minutes but to no avail. The ground was silent.

Suddenly, he jumped back with a gasp of shock. His chest heaved viciously, and his eyes were so wide he felt they would burst out of their sockets.

As soon as his heartbeat settled and his breathing steadied, he shifted to his knees again. Leaning forward, carefully, he listened. Seconds passed before he heard it again. A quick, scuffling noise penetrated his ears. It was the sound of a human fingernail scraping wood, he was sure.

*Chime.*

The bell.

*Chime.*

Moments later, another scratch.

*Scrape.*

*Chime.*

*Chime.*

*Scrape.*

*Chime.*

Soon, the scratches beat steadily to the rhythm of his heart. The bell was ringing frantically, but the rope attached to the hand of the person below still wasn't moving. Lester got to his feet and tried to run, intending to find a shovel and rescue the trapped mortal.

He couldn't move, frozen in fear by what he heard next. It was another bell, from the other side of the cemetery.

*Chime.*

Then, he heard another bell, from another direction.

*Chime.*

Another.

*Chime.*

More.

*Chime. Chime.*

No, these bells were ringing too randomly and frequently to be caused by the rhythmic patterns of wind.

*Chime. Chime.*

The bells were ringing even louder now, violently.

*Chime! Chime! Chime!*

Somehow, all of the bells in the graveyard were ringing in different tones, as if part of an orchestra. Terrified, Lester tried to make sense of it all. He heard no screams. The only sounds were that of scrapes, chimes, and rain.

He turned and ran through the foggy woods to his village, leaving the chorus of bells behind him. As he fled, he couldn't discern which noise was pounding in his head—the beat of his heart, the rhythm of his footsteps, or the chorus of the bells.

# 4

Soon, Lester spotted a cottage in the distance at the cusp of a new trail. Gasping, he nearly collapsed when he finally reached the door. Lester hollered and knocked until his throat and knuckles felt as numb as his legs.

An aged, grizzly man opened the door with a ferocious expression. He was holding a lit candle.

"You woke me, lad!"

"My gravest apologies, sir," Lester said. "Please, you have to come to the cemetery. Gather all of the townsfolk, and meet me at the start of the wooded trail. The dead have awakened!"

Lester didn't wait to see the man's reaction. He bolted down the pathway. When he finally reached his homestead, he decided not to wake his ironfisted father. Not even a graveyard full of dead ringers were worth the trouble of that. Instead, he hurried to the barn and grabbed a pitchfork before dashing down the path to join the fray. Even in his haste, he could not shake the eerie sound of bells reverberating in his mind.

Spotting a group of torches at the clearing before the woods, Lester slowed his pace and caught his breath. He prepared to lead his neighbors into a cemetery full of the undead.

"This better be good, boy," said the grizzly man. "You ain't better be wakin' us for nothin'."

Swallowing his nerves and regret, Lester mustered up his courage and said, "Follow me."

He led the townsfolk, armed with pitchforks and revolvers, through a winding trail of branches and rocks. The storm had passed, leaving a peacefully clear night.

"So, what're we lookin' for?" asked one of the villagers when they reached the graveyard.

Lester stared, bewildered by the scene before him. It was the opposite of what he imagined. The cemetery was quiet and calm, not a single unearthly noise. There were no chimes, no scrapes, and the only thumping heartbeat was his own.

"It happened," he said. "I swear to you. The bells were ringing, and the dead were waking. I heard it. I swear."

Lester looked around at the other villagers, hoping for support. Each stared back at him with an expression of frustration and disbelief. Some shook their heads, but all lowered their pitchforks. In unison, the villagers turned to commence the long walk home before dawn.

Hours later, as the sun boldly peeped over the horizon, Lester was still in the graveyard examining each bell. He searched for a possible explanation. The noises he heard were real, he was certain. He stood alone, until a pair of footsteps thumped towards him. He turned, foolishly hoping to see a walking corpse. Instead, the figure approaching him was the grizzly man he'd awakened from slumber.

"Just wait 'til your father hears 'bout this," the man said.

He grabbed Lester by the arm and pulled him towards the path. Glancing back one last time, Lester only saw a peaceful cemetery marked by uninterrupted graves. Hanging his head in shame, he resolved to follow the villagers back to an inevitably unwelcome reunion in town.

Creeping through the last hurdle of rocks, Lester and his detractor neared the edge of the woods when he heard it.

*Chime.*

# About The Author

Natalie Walker is a contributing author to the Storyshares library.

# About The Publisher

Story Shares is a nonprofit focused on supporting the millions of teens and adults who struggle with reading by creating a new shelf in the library specifically for them. The ever-growing collection features content that is compelling and culturally relevant for teens and adults, yet still readable at a range of lower reading levels.

Story Shares generates content by engaging deeply with writers, bringing together a community to create this new kind of book. With more intriguing and approachable stories to choose from, the teens and adults who have fallen behind are improving their skills and beginning to discover the joy of reading. For more information, visit storyshares.org.

Easy to Read. Hard to Put Down.

www.ingramcontent.com/pod-product-compliance
Lightning Source LLC
Chambersburg PA
CBHW071231170626
46809CB00005BA/2025